TODAY INFORMS TOMORROW

From the Students at
North Miami Senior High
Home of the Pioneers

Written by
Dr. Judith Grey's
Eleventh Graders
2021/2022

TODAY INFORMS TOMORROW
From the Students at North Miami Senior High
Home of the Pioneers
Written by Dr. Judith Grey's Eleventh Graders 2021/2022

Web: www.GoPublishYourBook.com
E-mail: info@GoPublishYourBook.com

ISBN-13: 978-1-941901-44-1 - (trade paperback)
ISBN-10: 1-941901-44-1 - (trade paperback)
ISBN-13: 978-1-941901-45-8 - (Ebook)

First American Paperback Edition: May 2022

CONTENTS

Every School, Every Student, Every Day

FOREWORD
by Dr. Judith Grey

This is Dr. Judith Grey, English Through ESOL teacher and a proud educator at North Miami Senior High School located in North Miami, Florida. The influx of immigrants to the U.S. has driven the growth of English language learners and the need for educators who are skilled in teaching this unique group of learners. I am grateful to be the teacher of such a group of children. All my students are unique individuals who come to my class with both strengths and weaknesses. We all have something to teach and something to learn. The authors of this book are my eleventh-grade students who were inspired by me to tell the world how they feel about the genres they were exposed to as a part of their narrative.

These high school juniors have been placed in my care for the 2021-2022 school year. Throughout this year, the literature they were exposed to led to the topics and writings of this informational piece. Students were passionate about what they were learning, and so, after many heated discussions, many hurts and disappointments, as well as AHA moments, I threw out the idea of spilling the emotions on paper. Hence compiling students' writing into a published book. Students selected their own topic and started writing in October and completed it in March. It was indeed a long winding road with some potholes but eventually some students were able to journey home.

Knowing that history informs the future, it was important that the authors relay their prominent messages. This book tells the stories of several authors trying to understand their history and why things are the way they are.

Looking at yesterday can help make plans for tomorrow. It was necessary for the high schoolers to bring awareness to their peers and others as they share new knowledge learned. This book will bring back memories that seemed to be short lived or forgotten.

DR. JUDITH GREY

ADMINISTRATIVE STAFF

North Miami Senior High
Home of the Pioneers

Patrick Lacouty | Principal

Steven Hoskins | Assistant Principal

Enock Alouidor | Assistant Principal

Lashawn Gaskin | Assistant Principal

Elvira Ruiz-Carrillo | Vice Principal

North Miami Senior High
Home of the Pioneers

Dr. Judith Grey's Eleventh Graders
2021/2022

Chapter One

FREEDOM OF SPEECH

by Emerson Torres

TODAY INFORMS TOMORROW

What is freedom of speech? People are trying to know what's freedom of speech. Well, it's a principle that supports the freedom an individual or a community use to articulate their opinions and ideas without fear of retaliation, censorships, or legal sanction. A lot of countries have constitutional law that protect free speech that's the definition of freedom of speech. The right to freedom of expression has been recognized as a human right for the people and the union. Many countries have constitutional law that protect free speech. People need freedom of speech.

Freedom of Speech and expression, therefore, may not be recognized as being absolute. People have the right to have freedom of speech. You have the right to Freedom of Speech. It is something that you fight for and keep on fighting, fighting, fighting, fighting. For your right to speak people think freedom of speech is not for everyone but everyone needs freedom of speech. Hispanic, African American, everyone needs the right to speak. We are fighting for It. Some people don't understand how hard it is, We the people are experiencing the pain; fighting, making speeches for our people, our family, and the children.

We the people have so many things to love about our freedom but there's always some people who try to take that love from us. We the people need to fight for our right, the right of our nation, we need hope to fight, hope to speech outlet for our freedom of speech. We need protection all of us we are all the same lovely, amazing people. We the people have to come together and fight and keep on fighting. We the people always have to be protected by the government. We pay for our taxes and our bills. We all need protection.

Listen to the things that we have to say for our freedom of speech. We need justice, and peace. This has been going on for years. This Is our American history. We the people believe that we all should have the right to speak although we all have different skin colors.

Need justice and peace! African Americans don't have freedom of speech. They are still fighting for it. We go out the world and try to fight for our freedom.

We have been going through a lot of pain. We lose family members because still to this day we are fighting and fighting for this moment.

All this hate that they got for African Americans will have to stop. Why do you need to hate when we are fighting for our freedom of speech.

We work hard. One thing that I'm telling the people is to always be safe, always fight for the freedom that everyone really need to fight for. Think about what I'm trying to say. We all trying to have the same freedom that Americans have.

Everyone needs the same rights. Fight together make America great again. Remember never give up for the thing that you are fighting for.

Don't let people stop you from keep going. Don't let anybody tell you what to do.

Thank you all

We need freedom of speech
Fight together stay strong together

TODAY INFORMS TOMORROW

Chapter Two
SELF DETERMINATION

by Alicia Thimo

TODAY INFORMS TOMORROW

What is self-determination?

The one thing people from all walks of life have in common is the ability to dream. There is no right or wrong dream, some people might dream of being a champion boxer. A person might wonder if everybody has a goal why more people did not accomplish their goal? Well, having goals is the easy part. Accomplishing your goal is the hard part, life always throws distractions, and setbacks in people's way. What separates people is their will to stop at nothing to achieve their goals. A person's self-determination in a difficult situation can have an overwhelmingly positive impact on being happy, by using failures in life to fuel one's desire to achieve their goals, by having supreme confidence in their abilities, and by not giving up on one's dream despite possible setbacks in life.

In psychology, self- determination is an important concept that refers to each person's ability to make choices and manage their own life. This ability plays an important role in psychological health and well-being. Self-determination allows people to feel that they have control over their choices and lives.

Chapter Three

WHAT MAKES A NATION

by Androune Eugene

TODAY INFORMS TOMORROW

What is a nation? A nation is people, history, government, nature, and tradition. When people think of a nation they think of a country, State, and land. But that is not all it is. To build a nation and make a nation takes a lot of work.

What really is a nation? - A nation is a collective identity formed by the various features of people that are collectively known as them. These features include language, history, culture, and/or territory. Some nations are referred to as ethnic groups, while others are associated with an affiliation with a political or social constitution. A nation is made up of the landmass that lies within given boundaries and is ruled by a government. In social science terms, a nation is made up of people who feel connected to one another because of some shared characteristic or characteristics. Some people like Paul James and Benedict Anderson both saw a nation as an imagined community. But For James, it is an abstract community, while Anderson sees it as an imagined community. In most cases, members of a nation are strangers to one another, and they will never meet.

To make a nation you need: land, population, government, tradition, food, culture, language, and law. First government, to have a notation government, plays a significant factor. We need someone to run the nation. The government. Control the army, policy and collect taxes. We need a government that can lead people and help people. Government makes laws to protect people and help people. Law like freedom of speech, and freedom of religion is important because people have a right to have an opinion and practice their religion. We need laws to protect us because the world would go into chaos. People would do what they like without consequences.

Next is tradition and culture. Every nation has tradition and culture. Having tradition is important, you pass it down to the next generation. Tradition refers to beliefs, objects or customs performed believed through the past. Traditions like Thanksgiving and Christmas are passed through generations. A Lot of traditions include culture. Culture is the customs, arts, social institutions, and achievements of a particular nation, people, or other social group. Having culture in a nation, it is important to bring people together.

But can a nation be successful? A successful nation will let the people choose their leaders, speak out without fear, and make elections honest and fair. A successful nation's gross domestic product (GDP) will rise over time, making their income rise. They use their resources and location to promote economic growth. It has safe food, clean drinking water, and good medical care. The primary objective of nation-building is to make a violent society peaceful. Security, food, shelter, and basic services should be provided first. Economic and political objectives can be pursued once these first-order needs are met.

Chapter Four
FREEDOM OF SPEECH

by Angelica Tarte

TODAY INFORMS TOMORROW

Imagine living a life where you cannot say what you want or express your feelings. Freedom of speech is a basic human right. Humans should have the power or right to act, speak or think as one wants without restraint.

Sometimes it is very painful to listen to people using your own words. Being a black human is tough, however I am not the right person to talk about what black people had suffered and is still suffering. Freedom of speech is a principle that supports the freedom of individuals or a community to articulate their opinions and ideas without fear of retaliation censorship or legal sanction.

The first Amendment to the United States constitution has been interpreted to mean that you are free to say whatever you want, and you are free to not say anything at all. Sometimes people are scared to express their feelings, it can be with your parents, your friends, or your teacher, you are not able to say what you feel, or to tell everyone how you feel.

In our century, people can express themselves through many other things rather than speaking with their mouths. People use the internet as their microphone to talk aloud what people whisper.

As a teenager I do have a journal where I express myself, where I show myself who I really am, and it really feels good after a bad or good day at school I can say what I feel like expressing.

What freedom of speech means to me? It's the key to be who you are by your own voice.

Chapter Five

THE VIEWS OF GOVERNMENT & DECLARATION OF INDEPENDENCE

by Jessica Anasthase

TODAY INFORMS TOMORROW

This writing is about the views of the government before the declaration of independence indeed their views.

The line between historical obscurity and fame is often a fine one. It's not surprising then that on July 4th no one thinks about the most important document produced by Congress before the Declaration of Independence: The Declaration of the Causes and of the Necessity of Taking Up Arms. As its title implies, it was a justification for armed resistance to England's abusive treatment of the colonies, with a chronicle of outstanding grievances.

Like many such historic texts written "by committee" its authorship has been the subject of some curiosity. Roger L. Kemp offers the now accepted explanation in Documents of American Democracy: A Collection of Essential Works. On June 26, 1775, after Congress had scrapped the first draft by John Rutledge of South Carolina, it appointed to the committee Thomas Jefferson and John Dickinson, of Pennsylvania. Ultimately, Dickinson wrote the final version, incorporating content from a previous draft by Jefferson. Though that draft is held by the Library of Congress, an original draft, in Dickinson's hand, resides at the New-York Historical Society.

AHMC-Dickinson

The first page of Dickinson's draft, 1775. AHMC – Dickinson, John

Perhaps influenced to some extent by his Quaker roots, Dickinson favored a measured course of action and so Congress presumably intended for him to mollify Jefferson's more combative rhetoric. In fact, Dickinson's demeanor had previously led John Adams to reflect in his diary that "Mr. Dickinson is very modest, delicate and timid." He would also later oppose the Declaration of Independence, believing it was premature for such a drastic measure. Still, the Declaration of Causes suggests Dickinson's approach did not preclude defiance. After all, the title itself is indicative of its purpose: a defense of "taking up arms" by the colonies. Even excepting Jefferson's rebellious influences, the document was far from conciliatory. Among the more quotable of Dickinson's prose is

"Our cause is just. Our union is perfect. Our internal resources are great, and, if necessary, foreign assistance is undoubtedly attainable."

Long before the first shot was fired, the American Revolution began as a series of written complaints to colonial governors and representatives in England over the rights of the colonists.

In fact, a list of grievances comprises the longest section of the Declaration of Independence. The organization of the Declaration of Independence reflects what has come to be known as the classic structure of argument—that is, an organizational model for laying out the premises and the supporting evidence, the contexts and the claims for argument.

According to its principal author, Thomas Jefferson, the Declaration was intended to be a model of political argument. On its 50th anniversary, Jefferson wrote that the object of the Declaration was "[n]ot to find out new principles, or new arguments, never before thought of, not merely to say things which had never been said before; but to place before mankind the common sense of the subject, in terms so plain and firm as to command their assent, and to justify ourselves in the independent stand we are compelled to take."

TODAY INFORMS TOMORROW

Chapter Six

EQUALITY

by Jikael Rinvil

TODAY INFORMS TOMORROW

When people talk about the word equality, what comes to my mind is equal rights, we are all humans. We are not different from one another. Come to think of it, going back to the 1950's I do not understand why there was racism to begin with. We are all humans; our appearance might be different, but we are still humans with hearts and everything else. I am confused about why people are not treating each other equally when we are supposed to have the same rights and opportunities.

I am not a fan of racism and being racist is not going to get you far in life.

My mother always says the good you put out into this world has a way of coming back to you.

Whenever she would say that it makes me think about what about the bad you put into this world; will it ever come back to you? I don't think I'll ever know if I'm willing to find that out. However, I do believe that everything a person does is defined by who they are.

When you think about equality you tend to think about race. Either side is never on the same page for example, look at the situation that happened with George Floyd and how the country was shown how equality is being used differently in terms of your race. People need to understand to not judge a person by their color. I judge a person by their mindset and heart, and I feel like everyone should do the same. Martin Luther king fought for us just to be on equal terms and not for us Black folks to be above White people or White people to be above us Black and Brown people.

I feel like some people are treating people differently just to make their selves look good and that is very disappointing to know. Even my teachers are always saying treat people the way you want to be treated and that is a fact, if you are treating people nice, they will also treat you nicely and I think that's what people should be doing instead of trying to make their selves look good. Also, when you help a person out, do not expect anything in return, and in my opinion, being equal is something so easy for people to do.

It is just that people want to have power over others and that is messed up. People who are in power are mostly likely to control other people. Going back to the Black African history there was no such thing call equality for those people because they were forced to work, and they were struggling to survive all because of their skin color and if you went back to read the history of African books you would see that only Black people were working. The white people were the ones beating the Black people up and making them suffer. I think some of the black people tried to escape and they end up dying. Most of them were saying even dying would be better than living like this. Every-time I read the book, I think about how we even survived all that suffering. If I could actually do something about it, I wouldn't want to be equal with them because they never even suffer like we been doing for all these years. There are multiple videos on YouTube that even show you how unequal we are to white people and the community. There was this guy name George Bruno; he went to apply for a job and the manager there just judge him on his outfit and his skin color. Really, like why they have to do all those things and make him feel uncomfortable. Overall, I believe that we all will be equal someday.

TODAY INFORMS TOMORROW

Chapter Seven
EVOLUTION

by Michel Judssaint Son

TODAY INFORMS TOMORROW

Evolution is the change that an organism goes through to develop into different forms throughout the history of earth. Humans have gone through many changes throughout history to get to where they are now. The specific evolutionary trait that I am focusing on is human speech. During mankind's evolution, communication was done through pictures or cave paintings. With the evolution and use of the larynx which is used to produce sounds such as talking, singing, screaming, laughing, or crying, has become an important use in society today. Just imagine way back then when humans grunted or screamed to communicate thought to where we are now having intellectual debates and intriguing conversations in different languages across the world.

When we communicate, we use pressure and air from our lungs to then engage the larynx to produce phonation and vowels which translates to words with meaning. Being able to verbally communicate is such an important aspect of our society. Symbolically human speech has been used to stand up against oppression. For example, Martin Luther King used his powerful voice to fight against racism and segregation in the United States. Even today it is used to help other people of color or minorities whose voice/speech is not as strong as others. It is incredible to see how we have evolved for the betterment of our kind.

Chapter Eight

PATRIOTISM

by Marvens Lenard

TODAY INFORMS TOMORROW

Usually, we refer to our country as our motherland. This further proves that we must have the same love for our country as we have for our mother. After all, our country is no less than a mother; it nurtures us and helps us grow. Everyone must possess the virtue of patriotism as it makes us better.

In addition, it also enhances the quality of life of the citizens. It does that by making people work for the collective interest of the country. When everyone works for the betterment of the country, there would be no conflict of interest. Thus, a happier environment will prevail.

After that, peace and harmony will be maintained through patriotism. When the citizens have the spirit of brotherhood, they will support one another. Hence, it will make the country more harmonious.

In short, patriotism does have great importance in developing the country. It eliminates any selfish and harmful motives which in turn lessens corruption. Similarly, when there is a change in the government the country becomes free and will develop faster.

Rani Lakshmi Bai was one of the most famous patriots of the country. Her courage and bravery are still talked about. Her name always comes up in the revolt of 1857. She revolted against the British rule and fight for independence. She gave her life fighting on the battlefield for our country.

Shaheed Bhagat Singh is another name that is synonymous with patriotism. He was determined to free India from the clutches of the British rule. He was a part of several freedom struggles. Similarly, he also started a revolution for the same. He dedicated his life to this mission and died as a martyr for the love of his country.

Maulana Azad was a true patriot. The first education minister of India played a great role in the freedom struggle. He traveled through cities and created awareness of the injustices by the British. He united people through his activism and led India to freedom.

In conclusion, these are just a few who were patriots of their countries. They lived for their country and did not hesitate before devoting their lives to it. These names are shining examples for the generations to come. We must possess patriotism and work for our motherland to see it succeed. I am a patriotic American.

Chapter Nine
HOW TO SAVE THE WORLD

by Max Alfred

TODAY INFORMS TOMORROW

Earth is our planet and a most important need for the continuity of life. It is full of all the basic resources to continue a life; however, it is getting declined continuously because of some unethical behavior of the human being.

Saving earth is the most important social awareness which everyone must know about to bring some positive changes on the earth. In order to spread awareness among students, teachers may assign them to write some paragraphs or complete essay on save earth.

Our Earth is the most beautiful planet in our solar system. As far as we know, Earth is the only planet that has life. Before 500 A.D., man had a good relationship with Mother Earth. But since humans developed cities and industries, the modern lifestyle has changed. Man has been using and misusing natural resources up to the limit. Now we are tearing up remote corners of the planet looking for crude oil and coal, and our forests and wild animals are disappearing. Our environment is totally polluted: we drink polluted water, inhale air full of dust, and eat food with traces of pesticides and other toxic chemicals. Hence, we are suffering from diseases. As a result of human activities, the ozone layer has a hole, the sea is rising, and the ice caps of Antarctica and Greenland are melting. Now global warming is warning us that climate change is not a hoax and it is coming. Mother Earth is in danger; life on Earth is in danger. Let us come together to save our life-giving and life-saving Mother Earth.

The evolution of people and animals were only possible because of plants. We need plants for our food supply. Plants are the base of the food chain and the source of energy for almost all life on Earth. Just as our forests are sources of our lives. Forests are ancient, mature communities of plants and animals, with homes and places for thousands of species. Forests give us oxygen, food, shelter, medicines, fuel, and furniture. Forests protect us from the heat of the sun, and from wind, cold, and rain. Forests maintain the balance of nature, the environment, the climate, the weather, and the composition of the atmosphere. As a matter of fact, forests are our life. But what are we doing? We are destroying the forests, meaning we are destroying our life and our future. All the problems we face today are made worse by deforestation. If we are thinking beings, we must save plants and forests, because they save us.

We cannot say the Earth belongs to humans; living things were using it for billions of years, before our own species showed up just some five million years ago. Our Earth belongs to all living things if it belongs to any of us. But we overpowered many species and killed them for our use. Now thousands of species are extinct because their habitat is gone. As a matter of fact, these animals, birds, and insects have built a better environment for us, provided us with so many things: they are not just creatures, but the real creators of nature. We are here on Earth because they are here on Earth. If they are gone, we will also be gone. So, the only wise thing to do is to save wildlife and its habitat.

Through deforestation, urbanization, industrialization, and pollution, our environment is being destroyed. Flows of energy, nutrients, and other elements are disrupted. Global warming and climate change are the major threats to Earth and all human beings. Due to carbon dioxide and other greenhouse gases emitted by civilization, heat is building up in the atmosphere at a rate not seen for tens of millions of years. The cities are becoming "heat islands." Pollution is becoming a great killer. Levels of air pollution, water pollution, noise pollution, and food contamination are high. Human interference has brought nature close to destruction. Now we all must come together to prevent pollution and save the environment and humankind.

All these environmental changes are warnings of global destruction. Now we all must become aware of these consequences. The evidence is disturbing: we are destroying our Earth and environment. Let's try our best to stop all this. Change your unnatural lifestyle to the extent you can. Use a bicycle as much as possible. Don't misuse precious water and electricity. Do not use plastics when you can avoid it by planting more trees. Don't allow anyone to cut trees, save wild animals, speak out and write against polluting industries, ask the government to use non-conventional energy resources (wind, water, sunlight, and biomass). Make students and citizens aware of the importance of saving the environment, and the many things that we can do to protect the environment, forests, and wildlife.

TODAY INFORMS TOMORROW

The tiger is an important top carnivore, and the most beautiful animal on Earth, but it is on the brink of extinction. Only 1200 tigers survive in India. Let us come together to protect this majestic animal and return its land. It is the tiger's right to live on Earth; after all, Earth belongs to all living things.

The world of today belongs to humans. What are the rights of animals, birds, insects and other living things? NONE: they have no rights. But why? They are the original residents of this Earth. We have built cities and forced the animals to leave their homes. Then we made our cities dirty, overpopulated, and polluted. Industrialization gave us air pollution, dust, tainted water, noise, and garbage. Cities have changed into heat islands, changing the weather patterns around them. All these changes have upset the physical and mental balance of the cities' inhabitants. If we do not do something to change this, not even humans will be able to live in cities, let alone other creatures. So here I suggest an "Eco-Cities Project."

Global warming and unpredictable shifts in climate are global problems. They affect every creature on Earth and are caused by human actions all over the world. It will take global action by governments, on a war footing, to change the habits and beliefs and technologies that cause civilizations to emit greenhouse gases.

Save earth is a slogan used to spread awareness among people about the importance of earth and why we should save our mother earth. Save earth slogan motivates people to save earth and its natural resources to give our future generations a safe and healthy environment. Everything essential that we need today has been provided to us by the earth. Water, air, food, shelter, earth gives us all of it, sustaining our lives. But the problem is that we neglect the damages that we are causing to the earth, due to our own activities, though, they are going to harm us only. The most prominent threat to earth is pollution caused by several human activities. The slogan "Save Earth" tries to persuade people like you and me to take necessary steps for the protection of earth and its environment. However small the contribution is, it will definitely be the beginning of a change that we want to see.

Chapter Ten
DECLARATION OF INDEPENDENCE
by Meloveda Victor

TODAY INFORMS TOMORROW

What comes to mind when you hear or see about the Declaration of Independence?

King Georges III was a tyrannical King who did not think about the needs of the Colony. The Declaration of Independence should teach the King to remediate for what he has done to the people and teach him that you cannot change what you have done but change what you do for yourself to become a better person. The Declaration of Independence states three basic ideas: God made all men equal and gave them the rights of life, liberty, and the pursuit of happiness; the primary business of government is to protect these rights.

On July 4, 1776, the second continental congress met in Philadelphia, Pennsylvania, and adopted the United States Declaration of Independence. This explains why the Thirteen Colonies were at war with the Kingdom of Great Britain and regarded themselves as thirteen separate sovereign entities which no longer subject to British sovereignty. They took a step towards the formation of a new State. The declaration was signed by representatives from New Hampshire, Massachusetts Bay, Rhode Island, Connecticut, New York, New Jersey, Pennsylvania, Maryland, Delaware, Virginia, North Carolina, South Carolina, and Georgia. The Second Continental congress passed the Lee Resolution for Independence on July 2, 1776, with no opposition. The Declaration had been produced by the committee of Five.

Congress issued the Declaration of Independence in numerous formats after ratifying the text on July 4. It was first printed as a Dunlap broadside, which was widely disseminated and read by general population. A signed copy of the Declaration of Independence is on display at the National Archives in Washington, D.C., and is widely recognized as the official document. Congress ordered the unalterable form of the copy on July 19 and signed it mostly in August. The Declaration justified the independence of the United States by listing 27 colonial grievances against King George III and by asserting certain natural and legal rights, including a right of revolution. Its original purpose was to announce independence, and references to the text of the Declaration were few in the following years.

In his Gettysburg Address of 1863, Abraham Lincoln made it the centerpiece of his policies and rhetoric. It has since become a well-known humor statement. We believe that these truths are self-evident: that all men are created equal, that they are endowed by their Creator with certain unalienable Rights, that among these are Life, Liberty, and the pursuit of Happiness. The declaration was was written to ensure equal rights for all people, and if it had been written for a certain group of people, congress would have labeled it "rights of Englishmen."

Finally, on July 4, 1776, the Second Continental Congress issued the Declaration of Independence, which declared the American colonies independent from Great Britain. The Declaration of Independence was a formal declaration that the colonies would now be independent from the United Kingdom. Now, we are an independent nation and celebrate our freedom annually on the fourth of July.

Chapter Eleven

TOTALLY FREE

by Mitchela Metayer

TODAY INFORMS TOMORROW

As Americans, we have very strong feelings surrounding the idea of FREEDOM. But what does it mean to be free? How can most people experience freedom? Are there limitations to freedom?

FREEDOM means the condition or right of being able to allow to do whatever you want to do without being controlled or limited. "So many people come from all over the world to America to achieve their "American Dream. 'With this, freedom, and Liberty, they can achieve it without any limitations or being controlled.

According to our Declaration of Independence "We hold these truths to be self- evident, that all men are created equal, that they are endowed by their Creator with certain unalienable Rights, that among these are Life, Liberty, and the pursuit of Happiness."

But, as you know, with great power (in this case freedom) comes great responsibility. One of Newton's three Laws of Motion state that "For every action, there is an equal and opposite reaction." This is also known as the Chain reaction effect.

This can be applied to life in general. In this case, talking about freedom, yes, Americans can do whatever they want. However, what they do affect their consequences in the future.

If it weren't for the military, the United States of America wouldn't be United. We would not have our freedom and rights. They made the choice to sacrifice their lives to serve and protect our country.

In short, we have the freedom we have because we have earned it from the British. We had a choice whether or not to stand up against the British, and we did.

We need freedom because it involves our everyday lives. How we spend our money, how we earn it, what we say, what we do, what we believe, all of those are choices we make. And those choices come from freedom.

Being free is the ability to do whatever you want without limitations or controls. But, with those choices you make there will be a cost later on. We live in a world where we can make our own decisions at our own free will, not someone else's will.

America is structured on Democracy and a free-market economy. Everybody has a say and still has someone to look up to as a leader.

Looking back at our history, we fought for our freedom. We stood up for what we thought was right. So, sit back, relax, eat some food, watch some fireworks. Everybody has earned it. Long live the American Dream!

"From sea to shining sea...Let freedom ring!"

TODAY INFORMS TOMORROW

Chapter Twelve
FREEDOM

by Deberson Louis Jean

TODAY INFORMS TOMORROW

Freedom is defined by Merriam Webster as the quality or state of being free, such as: The absence of necessity, coercion or constraint in choice or action. Liberation from slavery or from the power of another boldness of conception or execution of political right.

Freedom is more complicated than being able to do whatever we want. Taken too far, that approach would lead to dangerous anarchy, every person for themselves! Certainly, freedom can mean the right to do, think, believe, speak, worship, gather, or act as one pleases, but only until your choices start to infringe on another person's freedoms.

Freedom is understood as either having the ability to act or change without constraint or to possess the power and resources to fulfill one's purposes. In one definition, something is "free" if it can change easily and is not constrained in its present state.

Freedom is something that everybody has heard of but if you ask for its meaning then everyone will give you a different meaning. This is because everyone has a different opinion about freedom. For some, freedom means the freedom of going anywhere they like, for some it means to speak up for themselves, and for some, it's liberty of doing anything they like.

Freedom is an innate right which humans have since their birth. Freedom is not something that can be touched, seen, felt, or reached. All this gives a vague idea about freedom.

What exactly does freedom mean?

Freedom is the ability to express myself the way I want to. There is no uniform on how my life should be. With freedom I can choose my own moral compass and make my own decisions. Being in a country with freedom means I can choose my own religion. With freedom I can say what I want.

Different people have different opinion, definition, and thoughts about freedom. In political sense, some talk about social freedom, some about personal independence and some define it as religious freedom. But the fact that everyone wants to be free, holds true in all cases.

Freedom for me is being able to go for a jog in the morning, or take my grandma for a walk, or drive to the store without worrying about being targeted by some cop or racist who doesn't know me or can't identify with me because we're different. Freedom is all about having the right to be different. "To me, having freedom is enough to make me happy because a lot of people in other countries don't have the freedom, we take for granted. I think if people realized how lucky they are they would have more respect for the veterans and more support for them. They fought and is still fighting for our freedom.

TODAY INFORMS TOMORROW

Chapter Thirteen
JUSTICE

by Rolls Petit Jacques

TODAY INFORMS TOMORROW

As human beings, we employ acts of justice in our daily lives, like when you allow the elderly man to take your seat on the bus or punish your son for misbehaving. Yet, when asked to define the term "justice," it is challenging.

What is justice? This may seem like a simple question to answer but for many today it is not. Individuals throughout society have their own distinctive explanation of justice. It is a word in which, to every person, has a different meaning. Although "Justice" has a vast list of meanings, it can somewhat be defined. Loosely, it can be defined as "the principal of fairness and the ideal of moral equity." (Schmalleger 6.0, pg. 706) Justice is at the center of every debate, involving our criminal justice system, because of its vast majority of definitions.

Although the definitions are vast and complicated, what justice means to me is being punished for a crime that was committed. Seeing that the offenders pay for what they have done. This so-called punishment usually entails some type of prison sentence or maybe even the death penalty. For many people justice has the same meaning. But is it justice if a person kills another because that person previously hurt his or her child, or what about someone else who killed someone accidentally or in self-defense? Is justice taking "an eye for an eye?" How exactly should the punishment fit the crime? These are questions that make society ponders which form of justice to agree with. Although I believe that punishment should fit the crime, I do not agree with it to the extent of "an eye for an eye." This scenario is not justice to me because two wrongs do not make a right. I believe a person should be fully punished for a crime, but there are certain ways to go about accomplishing this.

There are many different types of justice and many ways that the term might be defined. In some cases, people speak of distributive justice, or fairness of outcome in the way various resources are allocated. In other cases, people speak of decision making. Issues of retributive or restorative justice, on the other hand, they are concerns as to the proper way to address instances of injustice; and while many may agree that justice is linked to the motion of fairness, ideas about what is fair differ among various contexts. In fact, it is difficult to give a complete and adequate definition of justice or what it means to behave justly.

Such injustice is the source of serious economic, political, and social problems. Today, the main thing I want to focus on is discriminatory injustice, its causes, and its solutions.

Discrimination is found in education, housing, employment, voting, lending, and credit, land use, health care services, transportation, public accommodations, and government benefits and services. Discrimination is described as unequal treatment of persons, for a reason which has nothing to do with legal rights or ability. Discrimination is considered illegal by the federal and state laws of the United States of America. These laws prohibit discrimination in employment ability, housing, rates of pay, right to promotion, educational opportunity, civil, rights, and use of facilities based on race, nationality, creed, color, age, and sex. Discrimination always promotes or reveals unfair treatment of a person or group of people based on prejudice and partiality which could lead to emotions such as frustration and anger.

Discrimination prevents equal treatment, there, it hurts the society. Discrimination has existed for a long time, and it needs to be ended so that we could live together in peace with equality. The eradication of discrimination is not an easy task to accomplish due to the problems that arise from discrimination and the time taken to solve it. To eradicate discrimination, the help of every single person is needed. This is not a task for one person or a group of people to achieve.

Therefore, discrimination is considered or seen as a social injustice in our society today. And therefore, we should focus on injustice instead of justice because if we continue to turn a blind eye on the problems in the world, we'll be blind to the justices we do celebrate which will make those justices be for nothing.

TODAY INFORMS TOMORROW

54

Chapter Fourteen
LIBERTY

by Judner Poly

TODAY INFORMS TOMORROW

Liberty is the ability to do as one pleases, or a right or immunity enjoyed by prescription or by grant (i.e., privilege). It is a synonym for the word freedom. In modern politics, liberty is the state of being free within society from control or oppressive restrictions imposed by authority on one's way of life, behavior, or political views. The exercise of liberty is subject to capability and limited by the rights of others. Thus, liberty entails the responsibly use of freedom under the rule of law without depriving anyone else of their freedom. Freedom is broader in that it represents a total lack of restraint or the unrestrained ability to fulfil one's desires. For example, a person can have the freedom to murder, but not have the liberty to murder, as the latter example deprives others of their right not to be harmed. Liberty can be taken away as a form of punishment. In many countries, people can be deprived of their liberty if they are convicted of criminal acts. In the state of nature, liberty consists of being free from any superior power on Earth. People are not under the will or lawmaking authority of others but have only the law of nature for their rule. In political society, liberty consists of being under no other lawmaking power except that established by consent in the commonwealth. People are free from the dominion of any will or legal restraint apart from that enacted by their own constituted lawmaking power according to the trust put in it. Thus, freedom is not as Sir Robert Filmer defines it: "A liberty for everyone to do what he likes, to live as he pleases, and not to be tied by any laws." Freedom is constrained by laws in both the state of nature and political society. Freedom of nature is to be under no other restraint but the law of nature. Freedom of people under government is to be under no restraint apart from standing rules to live by that are common to everyone in society and made by the lawmaking power established in it.

According to the 1776 United States Declaration of Independence, all men have a natural right to "life, liberty, and the pursuit of happiness." But this declaration of liberty was troubled from the outset by the institutionalization of legalized Black slavery. Slave owners argued that their liberty was paramount since it involved property, their slaves, and that Blacks had no rights that any White man was obliged to recognize. The Supreme Court, in the Dred Scott decision, upheld this principle. It was not until 1866, following the Civil War, that the US Constitution was amended to extend these rights to persons of color, and not until 1920 that these rights were extended to women.

Chapter Fifteen
WHAT IS AN OPINION

by Jean Villiers

TODAY INFORMS TOMORROW

After research, I can say an opinion is a way of thinking about something or someone. Everyone in the world can have one because is something free, it also depends on you, your way of thinking and your personality. Now the definition is given so we can say that everyone has one so let us start with mine and let me say why I have it. My opinion, your opinion, our opinion matter, this is my opinion about opinion. It is the opinion of mine because every single person in the world is different from each other in many ways but similar in many other ways, and that is not a problem because similarity does not prevent any person from having their own judgment.

Opinion is a person's way of thinking, his own beliefs, or views about something big or small. For example, "Yes, I think chocolate is good and Yes, I think the government is corrupt" both are opinions even though they are different, but still they both matter. A big fact is that opinion is something that many people do not like when other people have it, because if we retrace in our history, we can see that not everyone in our beautiful country can express themselves freely because of many reasons. Because some agnosticism sometimes thinks only their opinion matter, or not every person in the low social class can think, or every color of skin (ivory, beige, senna, band etc.) can think because not everyone is equal. But after a lot of fight against those people categorically we can see certain changes. Those changes are possible because we did not let it go and despite everything, we expressed ourselves. So, we can see that even opinion can change other opinions. Our country really needs people to express themselves because lack of beliefs in conviction slows us down. I use such rude words because even in the speech of the convention of Martin Luther King speeches he said it, maybe in different words but in the same ways of thinking. To conclude after all I see in our society the only thing that I have to say is that Every life matters. Every opinion matters.

Chapter Sixteen
HUMAN RIGHTS

by Snie Joseph

TODAY INFORMS TOMORROW

What are human rights? Human rights are the basic rights and freedoms that belong to every person in the world, from birth until death. They are the rights to life, liberty, pursuit of happiness, freedom from slavery and torture, freedom of opinion, freedom of religion, or right to work and education. Every human is inherited with these rights no matter what gender, race, the economic status they belong to. Human rights make sure that every human gets treated equally.

There are five kinds of human rights: economic, social, cultural, civil, and political. Economic, social, and cultural rights include the rights to work, the rights to an adequate standard of living, including food, clothing, and housing, the right to physical and mental health, the rights to social security, the right to a healthy environment, and the right to education.

Civil rights are an essential component of democracy. They're guarantees of equal social opportunities and protection under the law. Regardless of religion, race, or other characteristics. A few civil rights are freedom of speech, freedom to vote, freedom against unwarranted searches of your home property, freedom to have a fair trial, freedom to remain silent in a police interrogation.

Political rights refer to someone's ability to participate in the civil and political life of the society and state without fear or discrimination, political rights give the citizens the right to equality before law and the rights to participate in political process.

In short, human rights are needed to protect and preserve every individual's humanity, to ensure that every individual can live a life of dignity and a life that is worthy of human beings. These are important means of protection for us all.

Chapter Seventeen
LEARNING FROM THE PAST

by Yeuli Del Leon

TODAY INFORMS TOMORROW

The past is very important for universities, colleges and schools. If education centers have good reputation, past students are in good position and feedback is good then students want to get admission otherwise not. For admission people learn about the institute from their past. Hence, I want to say that past shows the direct impact on present in case of education centers.

In my opinion, for arranged marriages past is very important. Before marriage all family members want to know about the past of the girl and boy. I think this is very important for a happy married life. I have seen many cases, in which people did not know the past of girl or boy and after some time the couple do not want to live together and get separated.

In many cases, present depends on past. For example, science is past, and technology is present. Technology depends on science. Technology is implementation of science. That's why I am very grateful for invention of science. Technology is not possible without science. For discovery of new technology researcher has to go through science.

If people want to know about any country, then they will have to study about that country. With the help of history, people can say whether it is a rich or a poor country. Learning of past is also very important to learn about the culture of that country.

Past is also very important because we always learn from the past. It does not matter, whether it is good or bad. Sometimes if we make a mistake and not make a right decision for future then we will be alert and will not make the same mistake again. In my opinion I would like to say that past has direct impact on present. For instance, if students do hard work in their studies, then they get good marks, reach to a higher position after study and find a reputable job. On the other hand, those who do not work hard remain in same position and do not have good job.

Finally, I would like to say people should not be discouraged and disappointed if they do not have bright past. Mostly people say past has gone. But we have present in our hand which we should try to make it better.

Chapter Eighteen
PEACE

by Charvens Sainteus

TODAY INFORMS TOMORROW

What is peace exactly? To common standards peace would be defined as a quiet or no war period. That is correct but it is just a part of the definition of peace, this is just about half of what peace is really about.

Peace is a give and take process, where one is being given to and another taken from. "What is bad for one is good for another" one of the many proverbs that I learned. There cannot be peace without a victim. I am not saying that peace is a bad thing, do not get me wrong I like peace, but I know what it takes to get peace. Even if peace was a bad thing there is nothing that can be done about it. There is good and bad, the fortunate and the unfortunate, that's how life works, there must be a winner and a loser. Both parties cannot win.

With peace there is no equality, the world was never equal and probably never will, but peace makes inequality more obvious. Do not lie, haven't you thought of yourself as superior to another, that is a thought that everyone has, even me. A winner will never consider a loser as his equal or rival, it would be absurd. Let us take for example the treaty of Versailles, which is considered as a peace symbol, for the peace to exist Germany had to be the victim. Germany was forced to give up territory to Belgium, Czechoslovakia, and Poland. They were forced to become a republic instead of a monarchy, and its citizens were humiliated by their nation's bitter loss.

Then World War II (WW2) began and the treaty of Versailles played a part in it. Germany wanted to get back the territory that they lost, but that was not going to happen because they lost once again and lost more territory. Do you think the United States of America or Russia would recognize Germany as an equal. No! And no, I am not trying to justify Germany's action. I used this as an example to show you that there is no peace without a victim.

That is the full meaning of peace. If you are living in peace right now be thankful for being one of the fortunate ones. What you were given was first taken. But that is the cycle of life.

Chapter Nineteen
FREEDOM OF SPEECH

by Lovena Jean

TODAY INFORMS TOMORROW

The First Amendment states that Congress shall make no law respecting an established religion or prohibiting the free exercise thereof; or abridging the Freedom of speech, or of the press or the right of the people peaceably to assemble, and to petition the Government for a redress of grievances. But it's essential to remember that not All speech is protected equally under the First Amendment, and just because you have a right to free speech doesn't mean your employer, for instance, can't fire you for something you say (unless your work for the government and then things get a bit more complicated).

Freedom of speech, the right to express an opinion without government restraint- is a democratic ideal that dates back to ancient Greece. In the United States, the First Amendment guaranteed freedom of speech, though the United States, like all modern democracies, places limits on this freedom. In a series of landmark cases, the U.S. supreme court has over the years helped to define what types of speech are and aren't protected under U.S. laws.

Well, I would say now people are very sensitive and touchy and say stuff if they feel attacked so many people don't say what they would like to say.

Freedom of expression is a fundamental human right. It reinforces all other rights, allowing society to develop and progress.

Freedom is a condition in which people have the opportunity to speak, act, and pursue happiness without unnecessary external restriction. Freedom is important because it leads to enhanced expression of creativity and original thought, increased productivity and an overall high quality of life.

Chapter Twenty
SLAVERY

by Hander Christo Gardouby Severe

Slavery definition: slavery, condition in which one human being was owned by another. A slave was considered by law as property, or chattel, and was deprived of most of the rights ordinarily held by free persons.

Slavery was started in Sumer where Sumeria is still considered the birthplace of slavery, which grew from Sumer to Greece and other parts of ancient Mesopotamia. The ancient East, especially China and India, did not adopt the practice of slavery until much later, until the Qin Dynasty in 221 BC. 2019

Slavery in ancient times typically came about as a result of debt, birth into a slave family, child abandonment, war, or as a punishment for crime. At the outset, the slave trade wasn't very popular and was certainly not a booming global business. Rather, slavers would often seek out a buyer who could use the specific skills of a slave, matching supply with demand on a local and personal level. According to historical texts, the lives of slaves in ancient times were typically better than that of peasants in the same era, as they had regular care, food, shelter and clothing. Slaves rarely attempted to run away unless their masters were atypically cruel.

The story of the American slave trade is the first chapter in the history of slavery where most of us already have some familiarity. Whether it be from graphic films on the transportation of Africans aboard slave ships or your high school American history class, most adults are aware of the origins of slavery in the United States. The long story of slavery has not yet come to a close as many, including children, still find themselves enslaved. The first slaves were brought to the Americas in 1619, when 20 men from Africa were brought to Jamestown, VA.

Historians are not sure whether this was the true beginning of the legal slave trade in the colonies. Indentured servitude already existed in the region. Roughly 60 years later, via the Royal African Slave Company, records show that the slave trade was booming in the British Colonies, and colonists began to acquire slaves in larger numbers. Evidence suggests that the main reason for this dramatic increase was a sharp decline in the availability of indentured servants.

Slavery is an appalling practice that has existed since the origins of human history. Although at many points in history, liberators have worked to free specific groups of people, the Abolitionist Movement was different, as it aimed to put an end to slavery as a practice.

Some of the first countries to do away with slavery as a practice were located in Western Europe, around 1500. Many European countries were careful not to use slavery in their homelands, but relied heavily on slaves to build their empires abroad. The next step in the abolitionist movement was the ending of the slave trade globally. Slavers who were caught transporting slaves across the ocean were tried in court, and those captured were set free. However, there were still large numbers of slaves already in place in the Americas, and the profitability of the work they provided made them a valuable commodity to their owners.

Sadly, even through the hard work of abolitionists all over the world, the end of slavery didn't come in the 19th century. Modern or contemporary slavery still exists across the globe, often in places you wouldn't expect. Experts estimate that there are roughly 40.3 million enslaved people currently in bondage.

There are many forms of modern day slavery, all of which involve people being forced to work against their will. This can take the form of prostitution, physical bondage, forced labor, human trafficking, debt bondage or simply being born into slavery. Researchers estimate that worldwide these numbers break down to 25 million in forced labor, 15.4 million in forced marriages, 4.8 million sexual exploitation and more than 10 million child slaves.

TODAY INFORMS TOMORROW

Chapter Twenty-One
POWER

by Olminaidine Laguerre

TODAY INFORMS TOMORROW

Power is the ability to do something or act in a particular way, especially as a faculty or quality. It is the capacity or ability to direct or influence the behavior of others or the course of events. In physics, power is the amount of energy transferred or converted per unit time. In the International System of Units, the unit of power is the watt, equal to one joule per second. In older works, power is sometimes called activity. Power is a scalar quantity. Power is related to other quantities; for example, the power involved in moving a ground vehicle is the product of the traction force on the wheels and the velocity of the vehicle.

The output power of a motor is the product of the torque that the motor generates and the angular velocity of its output shaft. Likewise, the power dissipated in an electrical element of a circuit is the product of the current flowing through the element and of the voltage across the element. Power is the ability to influence or change an outcome. Personal power is a source of influence and authority a person has over his or her followers. Where does a person get this power from? In short, the power is determined by his or her followers. Having power involves taking it from someone else, and then, using it to dominate and prevent others from gaining it. In politics, those who control resources and decision making have power over those without.

In social science and politics, power is the capacity of an individual to influence the actions, beliefs, or conduct (behavior) of others. The term authority is often used for power that is perceived as legitimate or socially approved by the social structure, not to be confused with authoritarianism. Power is essential to bring changes. In absence of power, changes can be made but however, lots of struggle and lots of efforts will be required to bring even a minimal change. If power is in hands, then it becomes easy to make, mend, break the rules and bring the changes. Power provides protection.

Chapter Twenty-Two
HUMAN RIGHTS

by Sylvianise Jules

TODAY INFORMS TOMORROW

The rights of the people is another phrase as saying freedom. It is how we fight for it, to make our own choices, especially as a black people. We did not have freedom and we were treated unfairly because we did not have freedom of speech and we had to fight to get our freedom. Everyone should have the right to freedom of speech as long as they are not a threat to society. Today we can say we have rights because of our ancestors who had fought for us to have the right we have today and be able to enjoy our human rights.

According to the Ninth Amendment (1791), the Constitution of the United States, part of the Bill of Rights, formally stating that the people retain rights absent from specific enumeration. The enumeration in the Constitution of certain rights shall not be construed to deny or disparage others retained by the people. Human rights include the right to life and liberty, freedom from slavery and torture, freedom of opinion and expression, the right to work and education, and many more. Everyone is entitled to these rights, without discrimination. Having right is not just having the right to do what you want it mean more then that because our ancestors had fought for it.

Human right is right that belong to an individual or group, it is to protect all people everywhere no matter your race or gender. Human right is a right to a fair trial, life, and other cruel treatment.

Chapter Twenty-Three
THE RIGHT OF FREEDOM

by Wide Jeune

TODAY INFORMS TOMORROW

The right of freedom allows Individuals to express themselves
Without government interference
Or regulations
Freedom is the right of one's right to express and
Communicate their ideas, opinions, and beliefs.
Freedom is understood as either having the ability to act
Or change without constraints
Or to possess the power and resources
To fulfill one's purpose.

Freedom is often associated with liberty and autonomy in the sense of giving oneself their own laws and with having rights and the civil liberties with which to exercise them without undue interference by the state.

Chapter Twenty-Four
TO BE FREE

by Carl B. Charles

TODAY INFORMS TOMORROW

The Word "Freedom" is often interpreted in different ways. In today's society, as people form their own visions of freedom, we take into consideration various specific subjects of study such as their background; their bodies, constraints… but do not take into account the similarities and differences of the term freedom.

Additionally, the term freedom is often interpreted as a public and collective statue and by the fact of not being subjected, of not having constraints, not of being dependent on someone or something. Thus, freedom is therefore seen as acting of one's own will; to live your life as you want.

But being able to do whatever you want without constraint can disturb the people around you or cause big repercussions. In order to prevent disadvantage, laws have been put in place to limit people in their actions and allow a good sense of balance.

When this is not the case, it is the freedom of the community as a whole that is in danger and requires the intervention of the actualities. Even, if people must bend to natural constraints, we are endowed with a reason, a capacity for reflection, a faculty of thought and therefore a free spirit. We are autonomous and should obey the law of reason. When we are faced with constraints, that is with extreme pressure-imposed on us and against our choice, they take away the of heart freedom. Thus Freedom: cannot be totally appeased in order to have a society, being grace or some are not disturbed by the unlimited extensity of others.

Chapter Twenty-Five
STEREOTYPES AND MICROAGGRESSION

by Gaetanne Cherfils

TODAY INFORMS TOMORROW

Stereotypes are made up beliefs of people from different races categories and backgrounds. Today stereotypes are looked upon as normal or as a way of dismissing racist remarks, it can be both positive or negative depending on how it is being applied or said. Did you know that you might have inattentively said something stereotypical about someone or something without realizing it? Due to stereotypes being seen as normal in the 21st century, a lot of the time people may say something sensitive or provocative because they feel entitled or allowed to do so. Stereotypes come in all forms such as Cultural, Religious, Gender, Social, and Racial. For example, by saying that "People from this race are likely to commit crimes," "People who practice this certain religion are hypocritical and naïve," "People from this country are horrible drivers," "This gender is more superior than that gender." These are all good examples of minor forms of stereotyping. Some things may seem very harmless but there is always an outcome due to the meaning of what was said. Stereotyping can play a major part in changing people physically and emotionally. By judging somebody based on their appearance alone can really affect a person's mental health and sanity.

Stereotypes are mainly targeted on minorities coming from low-income families or country that are going through a crisis or is financially unstable and politically unbalanced. This can sometimes be seen as prejudice if said in a negative tone. If you ever find yourself stereotyping someone of another race you should; hold yourself accountable, apologize, and think before you say something that might be insensitive towards them. Also, remember to STOP STEREOTYPING.

Microaggression is a term commonly used to voice one's anger or frustration which involves violence, or sometimes demeaning of a marginalized group. Microaggression is a form of generalized idiocy used to depose of someone or maybe something. Microaggression affects people part of the LGBTQ+ community as they are considered different and gain a lot of backlashes for being themselves. Another group that takes the toll of microaggression are people with Disability this is known as Ableism. Ableism is a form of discrimination towards people that are disabled or falls in the category of disability.

Microaggression can take the form of either an insult or compliment. An example of microaggression in compliments are asking a woman of color if the hair that is on her head is real, telling a person from another race that they speak good English though they are from a different country, telling a plus sized woman that you wished you had half of her confidence when wearing revealing clothes, telling a man that is part of the LGBTQ+ community that they are manly for someone that is part of that community. These are all believed to be a compliment as they seem harmless and "normal" though meant as a nice gesture these can be very offensive to the person that falls in that category. Always remember to think of what you're about to say before it exits out of your mouth, because you never know what that person is going through and how they would feel about what you have to say.

TODAY INFORMS TOMORROW

Chapter Twenty-Six
WHAT IS POWER, REALLY?

by Giovany Valbrun

A lot of people assume that power comes from someone with a big title which comes with authority and control and a belief in the form of supremacy over others. Others believe real power comes from crushing your enemies anytime you want but I truly think power can be physical or mental. I personally don't think power is only limited for someone with a title or position. Real power is when you're not afraid to put your life down for something you believe in, something you want to achieve, where you must sacrifice your sense of happiness or satisfaction for the world.

Power is Infectious

Once anyone in a friend group chooses to become more powerful, everyone around that person becomes more powerful. Because seeing someone that you describe as a weakling rise through hard challenges overcoming the pain, he was suffering from might open your eyes to do the same. Honestly, this is where being mentally strong comes in. Will you be able to last that changing faze in your life? Will you be able to evolve to the next stage? I truly don't know it up to the person to decide.

Real power also sides with the impact you have on people, and it increases as we show kindness to others. Being powerful is more about giving support than getting support. Contrary to what you may have thought about power, service is the highest form of leadership. Serving others is a key to sustainable growth. And it creates the kind of influence that truly powerful people wield— the kind that resonates and uplifts.

Chapter Twenty-Seven
THE OLDEST CIVILIZATION IN AMERICA

by Jose Gomez

TODAY INFORMS TOMORROW

What is the oldest civilization in America? For many years, archaeologists considered Chavín de Huantar as the oldest civilization in the American continent, it was not until 1997 that the Peruvian archaeologist Ruth Shady discovered the sacred city of Caral approximately 40 km from the current Peruvian capital, Lima. The Caral civilization is characterized by its appreciation for natural resources which were very present in its rituals, its construction methods were based on mud and earth to build pyramids.

The Caral civilization was one of the most influential civilizations that appeared after this, many of the architectural techniques were used in Machu Pichu itself. What was Caral's society like? In the Caral civilization and mainly in its socio-political system, women played an important role, they were also valued for the role of mothers who performed all this is known for the sculptures of mothers holding babies in their arms or breastfeeding as well as for the different crafts in which they tell more about their role in their society.

How old was Caral civilization? Experts classify Caral as the oldest civilization in the American continent with more than 5000 years old and that ended up disappearing due to a devastating climate change that made them abandon their main urban centers and despite being known as a civilization in great harmony with nature Caral civilization succumbed to severe climate change and its devastating effects.

The Caral civilization, considered by experts as the first civilization in America with a great appreciation for natural resources, a great knowledge of astronomy and construction, succumbed to a devastating climate.

Chapter Twenty-Eight
WHAT IS A NATION

by Nashcaelle Joseph

TODAY INFORMS TOMORROW

A nation is a community of people formed based on combination of shared features such as language, history, ethnicity, culture and or territory. A nation is thus the collective identity of a group of people understood as define by those features. A nation is generally more overtly political than an ethnic group. It has been described as a fully mobilized or institutionalized ethnic group. Some nations are equated with ethic groups, ethnic nationalism, and nation state and some are equated with an affiliation with social and political constitution, civic nationalism and multiculturalism. A nation also has been defined as a cultural-political community that has become conscious of its autonomy unity and particular interests.

A Nation is an imagined of community in the sense that the material conditions exist for imagining extended and shared connections and that it is objectively impersonal even if each individual in the nation experiences are subjectively part of the embodied unity with others. For most part, members of a nation remain strangers to each other and will likely never meet hence the phrase a nation of strangers is used by American journalist Vance Packard. The consensus among scholars is that nations are socially constructed and historically contingent throughout history. People have had an attachment to their kind of groups, traditions, territorial authorities, and their homeland but nationalism did not become a prominent ideology until the end of 18th century.

There are three prominent perspectives on nationalism primordialism which reflect popular conceptions of nationalism but largely fallen out of favor among academics' proposals that there have always been nations and that nationalism is a natural phenomenon with ethno-symbolism that explains nationalism as a dynamic evolutionary phenomenon and stresses the importance of symbols myths and traditions in the development of nations and nationalism.

We can conclude that a nation consists of a large group of people having a common origin, language, and traditions. The term nation could be used to distinguish large states from small city states or could be used to distinguish multinational states from those with a single ethnic group.

Chapter Twenty-Nine

THE EXPERIENCE OF THE PEOPLE

by Leyka Paul

TODAY INFORMS TOMORROW

The experience of the people in slavery days was the hard labor, the amount of food they would give them and the different horrible kinds of punishment they would have to endure. The slaves having to work every day from sun-up till sun-down was inhumane and if they had families, they would be separated from them.

The slaves had to live in crude quarters that left them vulnerable to dangerous weather and disease. If they did not obey, they will get punished, hanged, and sometimes they would get burn, rape, whooped and so on. They would get passed around from owners to owners who use them as prizes like gambling and in raffles that was what the slave people had experience during the slavery, and they could not even defend themselves because if they do, they will get more punishment.

Sometimes the slave owners would not feed them. For fun the slaves would dance and sing, and if they run away and get caught, they would get flogged, branded, jailed, sold back into slavery, or sometimes they get killed. When they were freed, they had a lot of problems due to what they went through. They had to deal with racial hatred and disease and death. That was the experience that the slave had to go through, and they were freed but at the same time it felt like they were not because they had to deal with racist people and could not get a job without them getting a hatred comment.

Chapter Thirty
FREEDOM

by Stanley Guillaume

Type of definition:
- Freedom is understood as either having the ability to act or change without constraint or to possess the power and resources to fulfil one's purposes.
- The quality or state of being free or at liberty rather than in confinement or under physical restraint.
- Exemption from external control, interference, regulation, etc.
- The power to determine action without restraint.
- Political or national independence.

Why is freedom important:

It's important because it allows for change in a society and the exchange of ideas. It is personal liberty, as opposed to bondage or slavery. Freedom is a condition in which people can speak, act and pursue happiness without unnecessary external restrictions. Freedom is important because it leads to enhanced expressions of creativity and original thought, increased productivity, and an overall high quality of life.

Example of Freedom:

A bird being let out of a cage.

Type of freedom:
- Freedom of association.
- Freedom of belief.
- Freedom of speech.
- Freedom to express oneself.
- Freedom of the press.
- Freedom to choose one's state in life.
- Freedom of religion.
- Freedom from bondage and slavery.

What has freedom given to us?

Freedom allows us to talk about what we want and explain how we can go about getting it for yourself. You can protest for what you believe is right and even if it's wrong you are able to express it. You can have a religion to follow what you believe in, not what you are forced to believe in.

ℭ ❖ ℬ

All thanks given to the efforts of Dr. Judith Grey.
An outstanding educator who nurtures students' creativity.

ℭ ❖ ℬ

Judith E. Grey has over 30 years of teaching experience in both the Caribbean and the United States of America. She is an expert in Adult Education and is currently an educator at North Miami Adult Education Center. Dr. Grey earned a Doctor of Education (Ed. D) in Educational Leadership, Master of Science (MS) in Educational Administration, and Graduate Certificate in Educational Administration from St. Thomas University in Miami Gardens, Florida. Dr. Grey also holds a Master of Science (MS) in TESOL from the University of Miami in Florida.

She is certified in the Florida Public School system and holds National Boards' Certification and Florida Leadership certifications. Her areas of research interest and expertise include school administration, multiculturalism, and parental involvement as well as technology integration in education. She is currently the president for The National Board-Certified Teachers of Miami Dade Inc. Dr. Grey is an effective communicator, a pillar of her community, a problem solver, and a strategic thinker.